CAMP FEAR

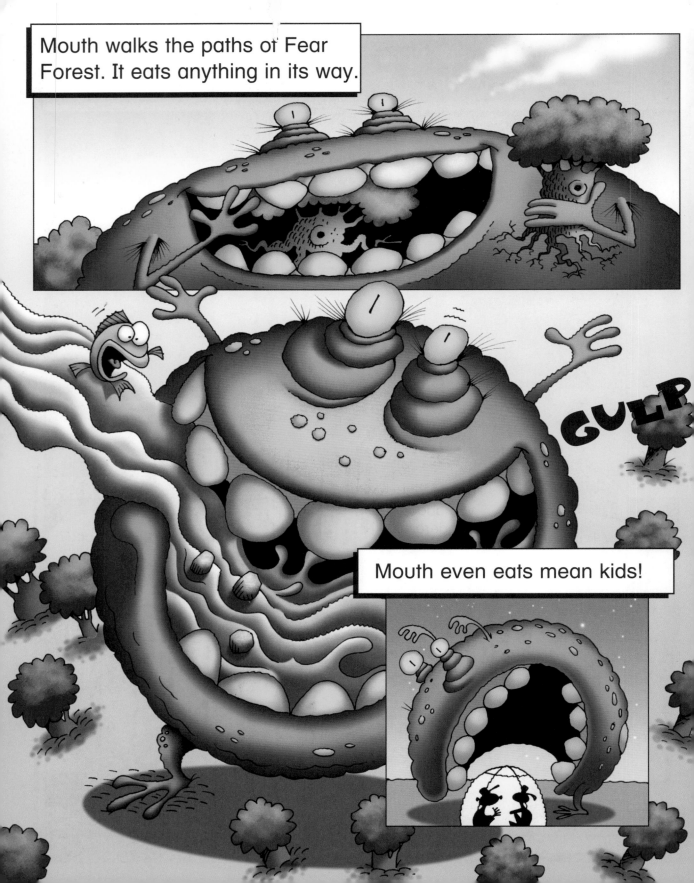

Thunderella makes huge storms.
It can make the wind blow.

BAM!

CRACK!

Thunderella can make
the rain pour down.

Thunderella can make it snow, too.

SPLAT!

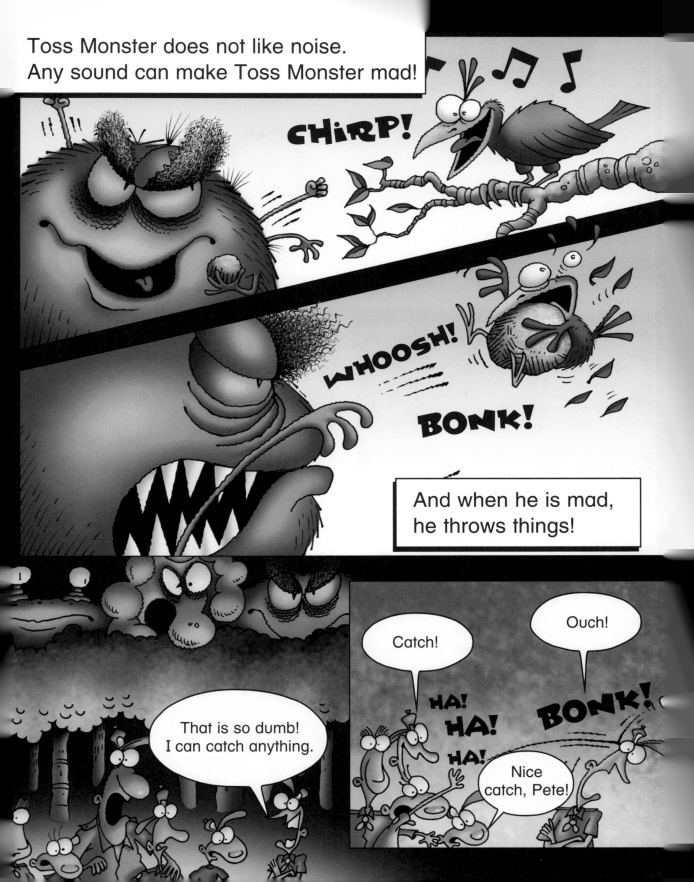

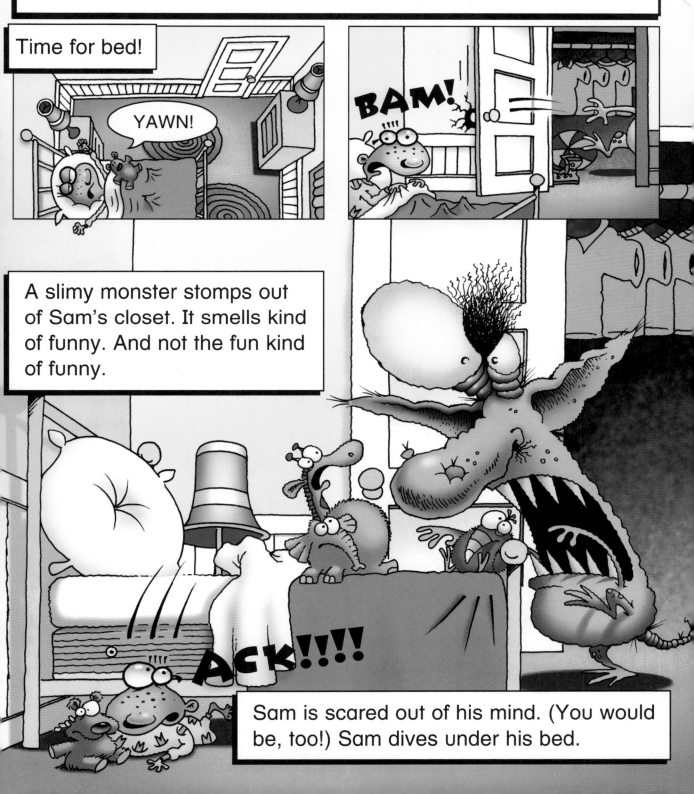

Closet Monster is ready for bed.

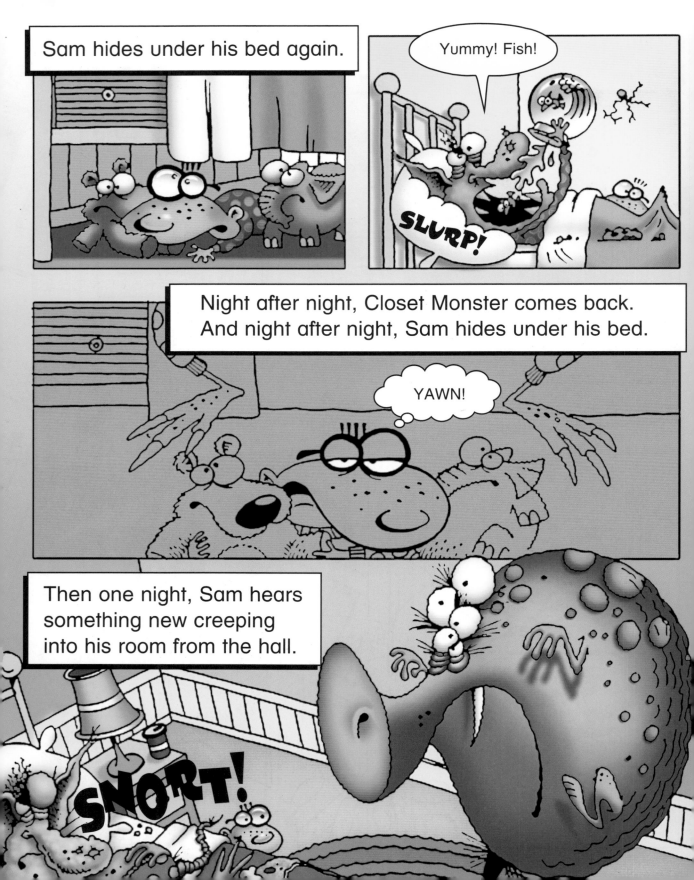

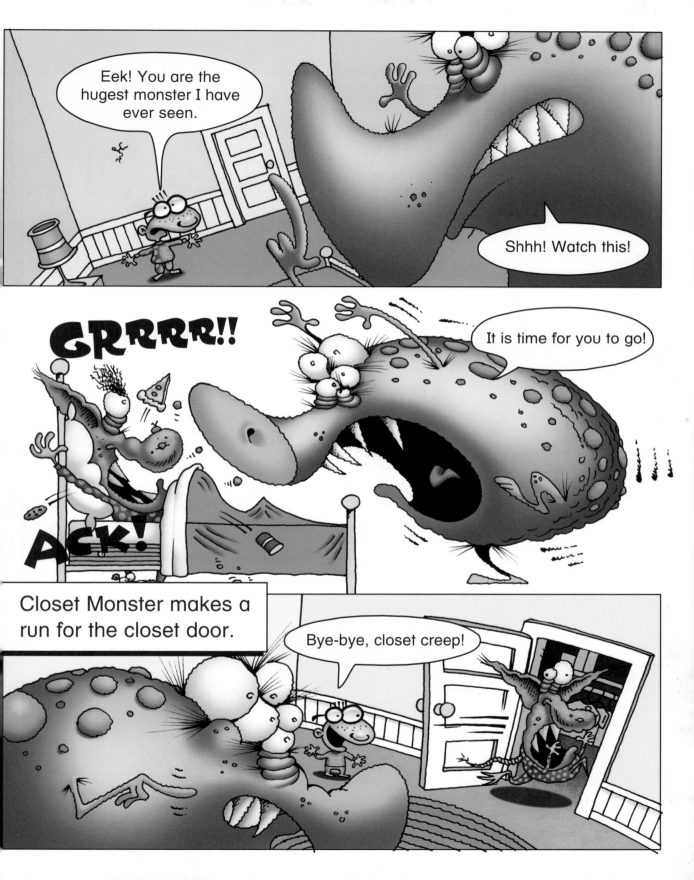

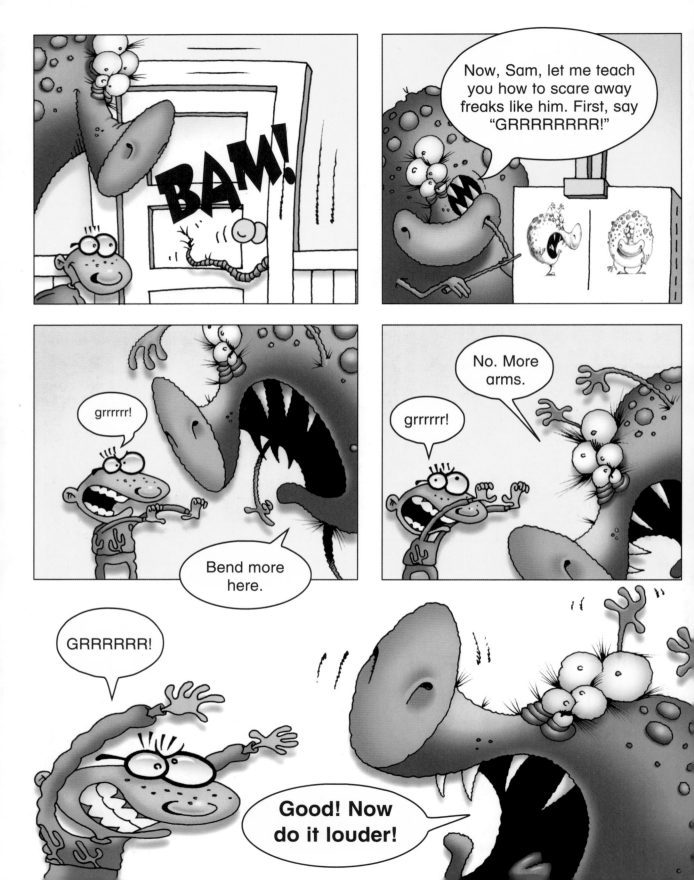

Sam is a fast learner.

Bye-bye, monster!

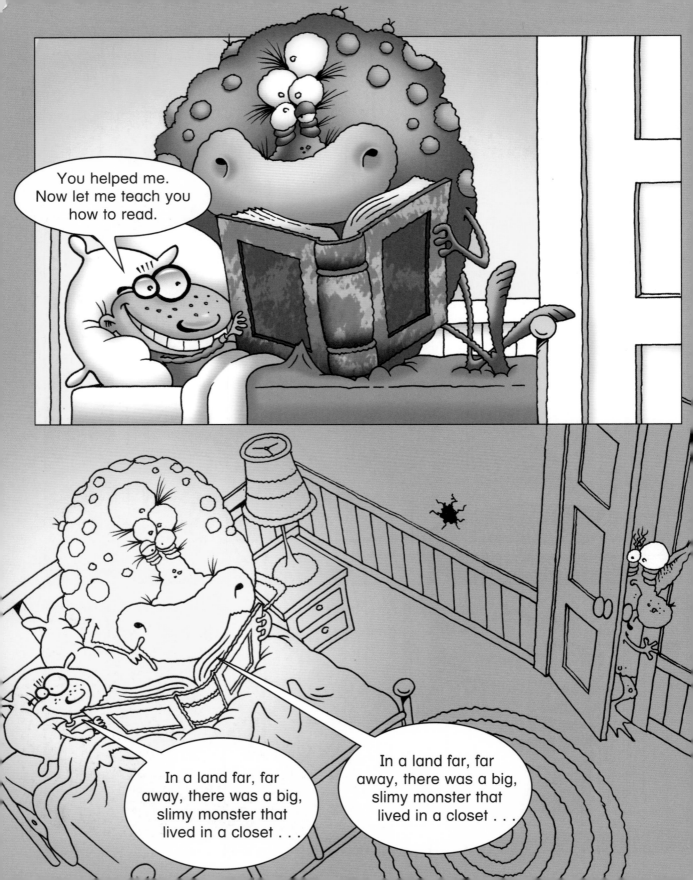

Max thinks he is done. But under the bed there lurks a huge, hairy dust ball!

No problem! Max knows how to clean up this mess.

I can get rid of you, dust ball! Kiss your fuzzy butt good-bye.

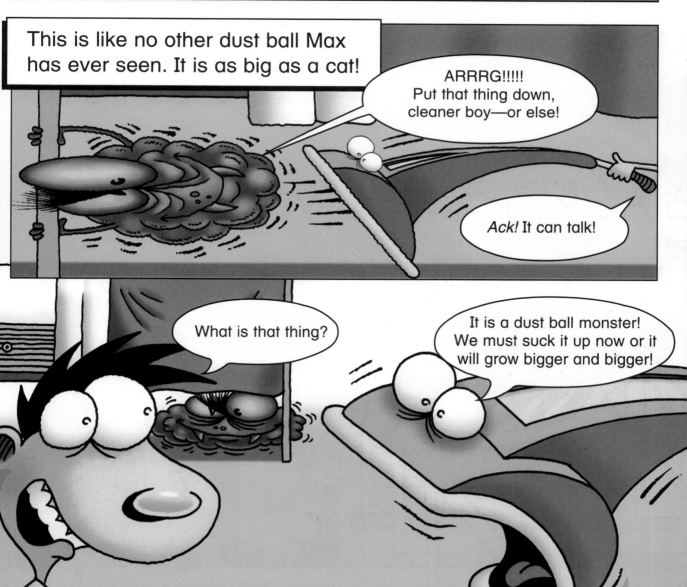

The race is on! The dust ball is in the lead.

You had better not even THINK about it, cleaner boy!

The dust ball monster takes the chase down the stairs to the den. Oh, no! Mom's glass frogs and bears are in there!

Watch out for Mom's . . . YIKES!

Want to dance, underwear face? Ha, ha, ha!

No way! You dance like a tornado!

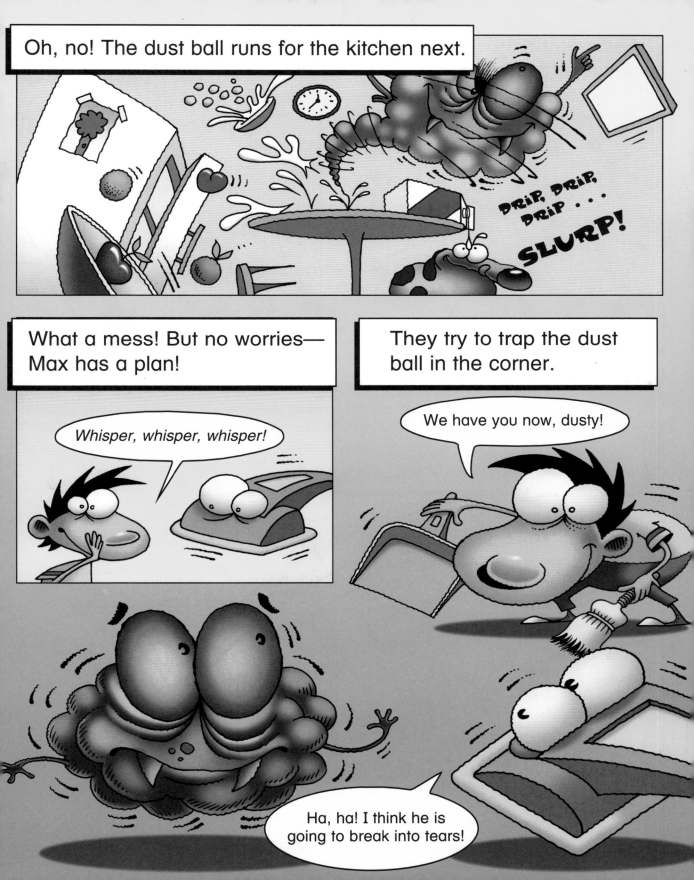

But then the dust ball grins. It does not break into tears. It breaks into lots of tiny dust balls! And they scatter everywhere.

The dust ball pulls itself together. Max runs for the bathroom and dives for the dustball.

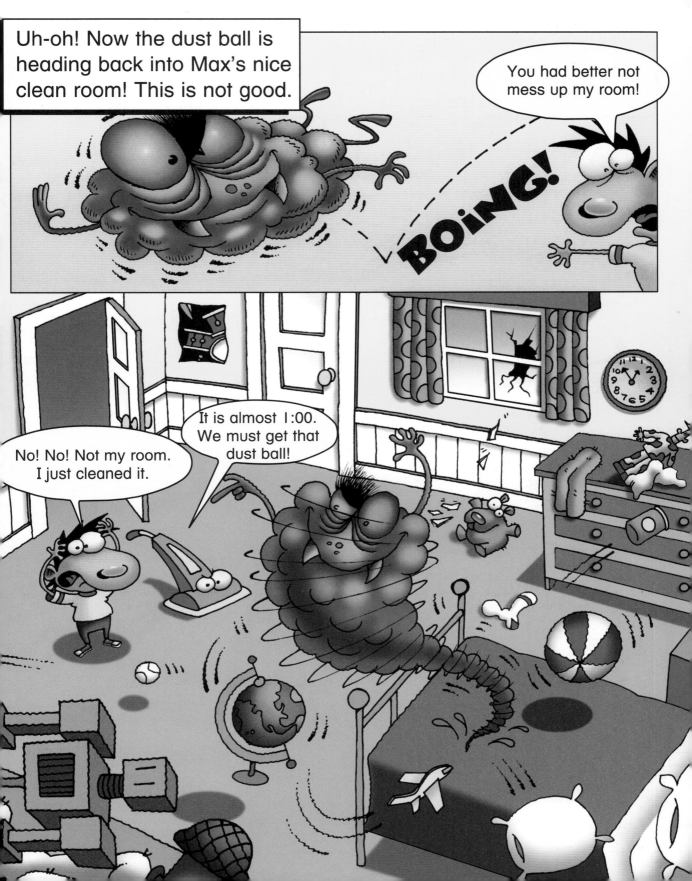